# The Specialist

By

Charles Sale

Illustrated by

**William Kermode**

PUTNAM & COMPANY LTD.
9 Bow Street, WC2 E7AL

*ISBN 0 370 00082 X*

*First Printed in England, February 1930*
*Forty-sixth Impression 1973*
*Completing 668,000 copies*

*Printed in Great Britain by*
*The Camelot Press Ltd., London and Southampton*

LEM PUTT—that wasn't his real name—really lived. He was just as sincere in his work as a great painter whose heart is in his canvas; and in this little sketch I have simply tried to bring to you recollections of a man I once knew, who was so rich in odd and likeable traits of character as to make a most lasting impression on my memory.                              C.S.

# THE SPECIALIST

# THE SPECIALIST

YOU'VE heerd a lot of pratin' and prattlin' about this bein' the age of specialization. I'm a carpenter by trade. At one time I could of built a house, barn, church or chicken coop. But I seen the need of a specialist in my line, so I studied her. I got her; she's mine. Gentlemen, you are face to face with the champion privy builder of Sangamon County.

Luke Harkins was my first customer. He heerd about me specializin' and decided to take a chance. I built fer him just the average eight family three holer. With that job my reputation was made, and since then I have devoted all my time and thought to that special line. Of course, when business is slack, I do do a bit paperhangin' on the side. But my heart is just in privy buildin'. And when I finish a job, I ain't through. I give all my customers six months privy service free gratis. I explained this to

Luke, and one day he calls me up and
sez: 'Lem, I wish you'd come out
here; I'm havin' privy trouble.'

So I gits in the car and drives out
to Luke's place, and hid behind them
Baldwins, where I could get a good
view of the situation.

It was right in the middle of hayin'
time, and them hired hands was goin'
in there and stayin' anywheres from
forty minutes to an hour. Think of
that!

I sez: 'Luke, you sure have got
privy trouble.' So I takes out my kit
of tools and goes in to examine the
structure.

First I looks at the catalogue hangin'
there, thinkin' it might be that; but
it wasn't even from a reckonized
house. Then I looks at the seats proper
and I see what the trouble was. I had
made them holes too durn comfort-
able. So I gets out a scroll saw and
cuts 'em square with hard edges. Then
I go back and takes up my position
as before—me here, the Baldwins

here, and the privy there. And I watched them hircd hands goin' in and out for nearly two hours; and not one of them was stayin' more than four minutes.

'Luke,' I sez, 'I'vc solved her.' That's what comes of bein' a specialist, gentlemen.

'Twarn't long after I built that twin job for the school house, and then after that the biggest plant up to

date—a eight holer. Elmer Ridgway
was down and looked it over. And he
come to me one day and sez: 'Lem,
I seen that eight hole job you done
down there at the Corners, and it sure
is a dandy; and figgerin' as how I'm
goin' to build on the old Robinson
property, I thought I'd ask you to
kind of estimate on a job for me.'

'You come to the right man,
Elmer,' I sez. 'I'll be out as soon as
I get the roof on the two-seater I'm
puttin' up for the Sheriff.'

Couple of days later I drives out to
Elmer's place, gettin' there about
dinner time. I knocks a couple of
times on the door and I see they got
a lot of folks to dinner, so not wishin'
to disturb 'em, I just sneaks around
to the side door and yells, 'Hey,
Elmer, here I am; where do you want
that privy put?'

Elmer comes out and we get to talk-
in' about a good location. He was all
fer puttin' her right alongside a jagged
path runnin' by a big Northern Spy.

'I wouldn't do it, Elmer,' I sez;
'and I'll tell you why. In the first
place, her bein' near a tree is bad.
There ain't no sound in nature so
disconcertin' as the sound of apples
droppin' on th' roof. Then another

thing, there's a crooked path runnin'
by that tree and the soil there ain't
adapted to absorbin' moisture. Durin'
the rainy season she's likely to be
slippery. Take your grandpappy—
goin' out there is about the only
recreation he gets. He'll go out some
rainy night with his nighties flappin'
around his legs, and like as not when
you come out in the mornin' you'll
find him prone in the mud, or maybe
skidded off one of them curves and
wound up in the corn crib. No, sir,'
I sez, 'put her in a straight line with
the house and, if it's all the same to
you, have her go past the wood-pile.
I'll tell you why.

'Take a woman, fer instance—out
she goes. On the way back she'll
gather five sticks of wood, and the
average woman will make four or five
trips a day. There's twenty sticks in
the wood box without any trouble.
On the other hand, take a timid
woman, if she sees any men folks
around, she's too bashful to go direct

out, so she'll go to the wood-pile, pick
up the wood, go back to the house
and watch her chance. The average
timid woman—especially a new hired
girl—I've knowed to make as many
as ten trips to the wood-pile before
she goes in, regardless. On a good
day you'll have your wood box filled
by noon, and right there is a savin'
of time.

'Now, about the diggin' of her.
You can't be too careful about that,'

I sez; 'dig her deep and dig her wide.
It's a mighty sight better to have a
little privy over a big hole than a
big privy over a little hole. Another
thing; when you dig her deep you've
got her dug; and you ain't got that
disconcertin' thought stealin' over
you that sooner or later you'll have
to dig again.'

'And when it comes to construction,' I sez, 'I can give you joists or
beams. Joists make a good job. Beams
cost a bit more, but they're worth it.
Beams, you might say, will last for-
ever. 'Course, I could give you joists,
but take your Aunt Emmy, she ain't
gettin' a mite lighter. Some day she
might be out there when them joists
give way and there she'd be—catched.
Another thing you've got to figger on,
Elmer,' I sez, 'is that Odd Fellows
picnic in the fall. Them boys is goin'
to get in there in fours and sixes,
singin' and drinkin', and the like, and
I want to tell you there's nothin'
breaks up an Odd Fellows picnic

quicker than a diggin' party. Beams,
I say, every time, and rest secure.

'And about her roof,' I sez. 'I can
give you a lean-to type or a pitch roof.
Pitch roofs cost a little more, but some
of our best people has lean-tos. If it
was fer myself, I'd have a lean-to, and
I'll tell you why.

'A lean-to has two less corners fer
the wasps to build their nests in; and
on a hot August afternoon there ain't
nothin so disconcertin' as a lot of
wasps buzzin' 'round while you're
settin' there doin' a little readin',
figgerin', or thinkin'. Another thing,'
I sez, 'a lean-to gives you a high door.
Take that son of yours, shootin' up
like a weed; don't any of him seem
to be turnin' under. If he was tryin'
to get under a pitch roof door he'd
crack his head everytime. Take a
lean-to, Elmer; they ain't stylish, but
they're practical.

'Now, about her furnishin's. I can
give you a nail or hook for the catalogue, and besides, a box for cobs.

You take your pa, for instance; he's
of the old school and naturally he'd
prefer the box; so put 'em both in,
Elmer. Won't cost you a bit more for
the box and keeps peace in the family.
You can't teach an old dog new tricks,'
I sez.

'And as long as we're on furnishin's,
I'll tell you about a technical point
that was put to me the other day.
The question was this: "What is the
life, or how long will the average mail
order catalogue last, in just the plain,
ordinary eight family three holer?"
It stumped me for a spell; but this
bein' a reasonable question I checked
up, and found that by placin' the
catalogue in there, say in January—
when you get your new one—you
should be into the harness section by
June; but, of course, that ain't through
apple time, and not countin' on too
many city visitors, either.

'An' another thing—they've been
puttin' so many of those stiff-coloured
sheets in the catalogue here lately that

it makes it hard to figger. Somethin'
really ought to be done about this,
and I've thought about takin' it up
with Mr. Sears Roebuck hisself.

'As to the latch fer her, I can give
you a spool and string, or a hook and
eye. The cost of a spool and string is
practically nothin', but they ain't
positive in action. If somebody comes
out and starts rattlin' the door, either
the spool or the string is apt to give
way, and there you are. But, with a
hook and eye she's yours, you might
say, for the whole afternoon, if you're
so minded. Put on the hook and eye
of the best quality 'cause there ain't
nothin' that'll rack a man's nerves
more than to be sittin' there ponderin',
without a good, strong, substantial
latch on the door.' And he agreed
with me.

'Now,' I sez 'what about windows;
some want 'em, some don't. They
ain't so popular as they used to be.
If it was me, Elmer, I'd say no windows; and I'll tell you why. Take,

fer instance, somebody comin' out—
maybe they're just in a hurry or maybe they waited too long. If the door
don't open right away and you won't
answer 'em, nine times out of ten
they'll go 'round and 'round and look
in the window, and you don't get the
privacy you ought to.

'Now, about ventilators, or the
designs I cut in the doors. I can give
you stars, diamonds, or crescents—
there ain't much choice—all give good
service. A lot of people like stars, because they throw a ragged shadder.
Others like crescents 'cause they're
graceful and simple. Last year we was
cuttin' a lot of stars; but this year
people are kinda quietin' down and
runnin' more to crescents. I do cut
twinin' hearts now and then for young
married couples; and bunches of
grapes for the newly rich. These last
two designs come under the head of
novelties and I don't very often
suggest 'em, because it takes time and
runs into money.

'I wouldn't take any snap judgment on her ventilators, Elmer,' I sez, 'because they've got a lot to do with the beauty of the structure. And don't over-do it, like Doc Turner did. He wanted stars and crescents both, against my better judgment, and now he's sorry. But it's too late; 'cause when I cut 'em, they're cut.' And, gentlemen, you can get mighty tired, sittin' day after day lookin' at a ventilator that ain't to your likin'.

I never use knotty timber. All clean white pine—and I'll tell you why: You take a knot hole; if it doesn't fall out it will get pushed out; and if it comes in the door, nine times out of ten it will be too high to sit there and look out, and just the right height for some snooper to sneak around, peak in—and there you are——catched.

'Now,' I sez, 'how do you want that door to swing? Openin' in or out?' He said he didn't know. So I sez it should open in. This is the way it works out: 'Place yourself in there.

The door openin' in, say about forty-
five degree. This gives you air and
lets the sun beat in. Now, if you hear
anybody comin', you can give it a
quick shove with your foot and there
you are. But if she swings out, where
are you? You can't run the risk of
havin' her open for air or sun, because
if anyone comes, you can't get up off
that seat, reach way around and grab
'er without gettin' caught, now can
you?' He could see I was right.

So I built his door like all my doors,
swingin' in, and, of course, facing east,
to get the full benefit of th' sun. And
I tell you, gentlemen, there ain't
nothin' more restful than to get out
there in the mornin', comfortably
seated, with th' door about three-
fourths open. The old sun, beatin' in
on you, sort of relaxes a body—makes
you feel m-i-g-h-t-y, m-i-g-h-t-y
r-e-s-t-f-u-l.

'Now.' I sez, 'about the paintin' of
her. What color do you want 'er,
Elmer?' He said red. 'Elmer,' I sez,

I can paint her red, and red makes a beautiful job; or I can paint her a bright green, or any one of a half-dozen other colors, and they're all mighty pretty; but it ain't practical to use a single solid color, and I'll tell you why. She's too durn hard to see at night. You need contrast—just like they use on them railroad crossin' bars—so you can see 'em in the dark.

'If I was you, I'd paint her a bright red, with white trimmin's—just like your barn. Then she'll match up nice in the daytime, and you can spot 'er easy at night, when you ain't got much time to go scoutin' around.

'There's a lot of fine points to puttin' up a first-class privy that the average man don't think about. It's no job for an amachoor, take my word on it. There's a whole lot more to it than you can see by just takin' a few squints at your nabor's. Why, one of the worst tragedies around heer in years was because old man Clark's

boys thought they knowed somethin'
about this kind of work, and they
didn't.

'Old man Clark—if he's a day he's
ninety-seven—lives over there across
the holler with his boys. Asked me to
come over and estimate on their job.
My price was too high; so they decided to do it themselves. And that's
where the trouble begun.

'I was doin' a little paper hangin'
at the time for that widder that lives
down past the old creamery. As I'd
drive by I could see the boys a-
workin'. Of course, I didn't want to
butt in, so used to just holler at 'em
on the way by and say, naborly like:
"Hey, boys, see you're doin a little
buildin'." You see, I didn't want to
act like I was buttin' in on their work;
but I knowed all the time they was
going to have trouble with that privy.
And they did. From all outside ap-
pearance it was a regulation job, but
not being experienced along this line,
they didn't anchor her.

'You see, I put a 4 by 4 that runs
from the top right straight on down
five foot into the ground. That's why
you never see any of my jobs upset
Hallowe'en night. They might *pull*
'em out, but they'll never upset 'em.

'Here's what happened: They didn'
anchor theirs, and they painted it
solid red—two bad mistakes.

'Hallowe'en night came along,
darker than pitch. Old man Clark
was out in there. Some of them
devilish nabor boys was out for no
good, and they upset 'er with the old
man in it.

'Of course, the old man got to
callin' and his boys heard the noise.
One of 'em sez: "What's the racket?
Somebody must be at the chickens."
So they took the lantern, started out
to the chicken shed. They didn't find
anything wrong there, and they
started back to the house. Then they
heerd the dog bark, and one of his
boys sez: "Sounds like that barkin' is
over towards the privy." It bein'

painted red, they couldn't see she was upset, so they started over there.

'In the meantime the old man had gotten so confused that he started to crawl out through the hole, yellin' for help all the time. The boys reckonized his voice and come runnin', but just as they got there he lost his holt and fell. After that they just *called*—didn't go near him. So you see what a tragedy that was; and they tell me he has been practically ostercized from society ever since.'

Well, time passed, and I finally got Elmer's job done; and, gentlemen, everybody says that, next to my eight holer, it's the finest piece of construction work in the county.

Sometimes, when I get to feelin' blue and thinkin' I hitched my wagon to the wrong star, and may be I should have took up chiropracty or veternary, I just pack the little woman and the kids in the back of my car and start out, aimin' to fetch up at Elmer's place along about dusk.

When we gets to the top of the hill overlookin' his place, we stops. I slips the gear in mutual, and we jest sit there lookin' at that beautiful sight. There sits that privy on that knoll near the wood-pile, painted red and white, mornin' glories growin' up over her and Mr. Sun bathin' her in a burst of yeller color as he drops back of them hills. You can hear the dog barkin' in the distance, bringin' the cows up fer milkin', and the slow squeak of Elmer's windmill pumpin' away day after day the same as me.

As I look at that beautiful picture of my work, I'm proud. I heaves a sigh of satisfaction, my eyes fill up and I sez to myself, 'Folks are right when they say that next to my eight holer that's the finest piece of construction work I ever done. I know I done right in Specializin'; I'm sittin' on top of the world; and I hope that boy of mine who is growin' up like a weed keeps up the good work when I'm gone.'

With one last look as we pulls away, I slips my arm around the Missus and I sez: 'Nora, Elmer don't have to worry, he's a boy that's got hisself a privy, a m-i-g-h-t-y, m-i-g-h-t-y, p-r-e-t-t-y p-r-i-v-y.'

The end